W9-CPD-930

HERO CAT

by
Eileen Spinelli

illustrated by
Jo Ellen McAllister Stammen

Marshall Cavendish Children

Marshall Cavendish Corporation, 99 White Plains Road, Tarrytown, NY 10591
www.marshallcavendish.us/kids

Library of Congress Cataloging-in-Publication Data
Spinelli, Eileen.
Hero cat / by Eileen Spinelli ; illustrated by Jo Ellen McAllister Stammen.— 1st ed.
p. cm.
Summary: A cat gives birth to a litter of kittens in an abandoned building that
catches fire while she is out searching for food.
ISBN: 978-0-7614-5223-2 (hardcover)   ISBN: 978-0-7614-5837-1 (paperback)
[1. Cats—Fiction. 2. Animals—Infancy—Fiction. 3. Fires—Fiction.] I. McAllister
Stammen, Jo Ellen, ill. II. Title.
PZ7.S7566Her 2006
[E]—dc22
2005007895

The illustrations are rendered in pastel.
Book design by Becky Terhune
Editor: Margery Cuyler

Printed in Malaysia (T)
1 3 5 6 4 2

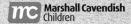
Marshall Cavendish
Children

To my mom, Lois McAllister
— J. E. M.

For Joan Donaldson, Margie Flintom, and Ana Baca
— E. S.

It was March. Cold and slushy. Time for Mother Cat to have her kittens.

Seeking shelter, she dragged herself into an old garage. "Hissss!" snarled an old tomcat, shooing her away.

Next she tried a back alley shed. "Scat,
cat!" said two boys who were trading cards.

At last she came to a dark, abandoned
building. No one was there to chase her.
Mother Cat lay down on some old rags,
with only her own breath for warmth.

Amid dusty machinery and empty cartons and rain puddling under the door, she gave birth to her precious kittens. Five of them.
Black-and-White.
Gray.
Siamese.
White Paws.
And Smokey.

Mother Cat nursed and cuddled them. She purred starry lullabies and licked clean their silky fur.

The days passed and Mother Cat grew hungry. She nosed her kittens into a cozy heap and left the garage to look for food.

After swallowing a few fish tails and some stale cheese, she hurried back.

Along the way she heard fire engines. She smelled smoke. Then she saw the flames coming from the dark, abandoned building.

The kittens!

Plunging through thick smoke, she ran inside. She heard frightened mewing.

There was Black-and-White, huddled against the wall. The kitten whimpered as Mother Cat carried her out the door.

She dropped Black-and-White on a wet patch of grass and raced back.

Hot boards scorched her paws. Smoke made her eyes burn. She found Gray and carried him to the sidewalk. Three kittens left.

Into the smoke and flames again.
Tiny cries.
Siamese . . . there . . . yes . . . out . . . safe.

The wind was rising. Greasy windows popped. Mother Cat went back. She heard crying in the rags that had been their bed. White Paws. Mother Cat lifted him with her mouth.

Safe at last with his brothers and sister.

Fire flared skyward. One more
kitten. Smokey. Heart racing, Mother
Cat returned to the building.
No cry. No scent.

SMOKEEEEEEEEEEE!

She stumbled into him. Tiny ball of
fur in the corner. Hardly breathing. She
carried Smokey outside, dumped him
with the others.
And collapsed, exhausted.

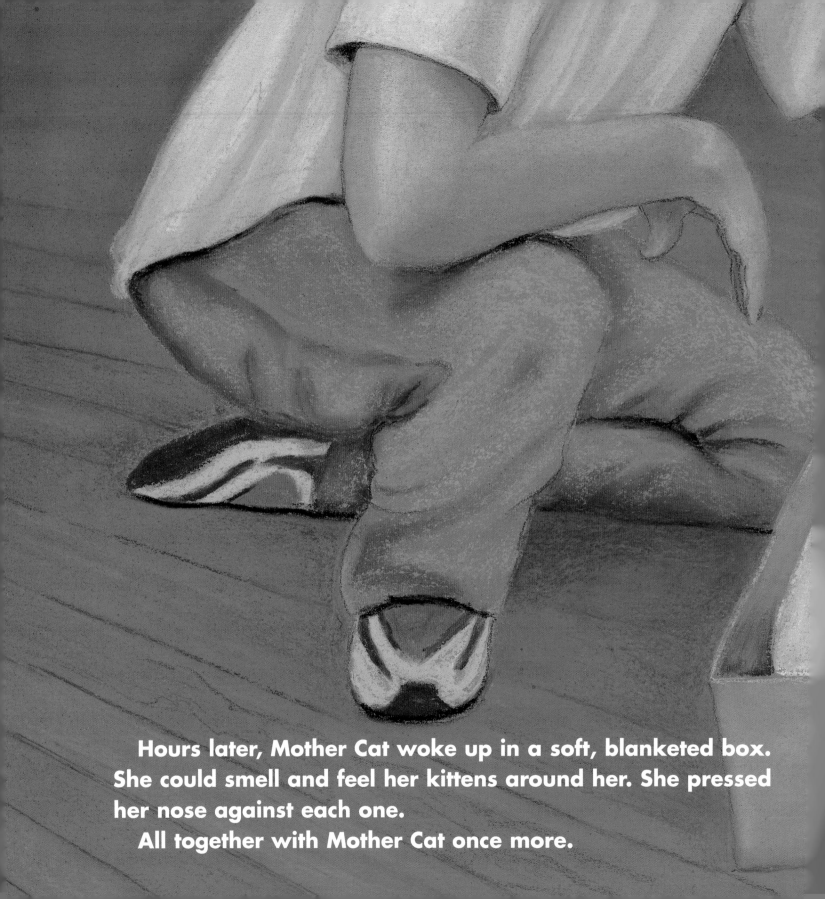

Hours later, Mother Cat woke up in a soft, blanketed box. She could smell and feel her kittens around her. She pressed her nose against each one.

All together with Mother Cat once more.

A photographer took a picture of them.

"Cute kittens," he said.

"Brave cat," said a firewoman.

A fireman knelt by the box and patted Mother Cat on the head. "More than brave," he said. "This cat is a . . . hero cat!"

AUTHOR'S NOTE

I was inspired to write *Hero Cat* after reading the true story of a homeless cat who rescued her kittens from a burning building in 1996. They were discovered by a firefighter, David Giannelli, who took them to an animal shelter on the North Shore of Long Island, New York.

When the cats recovered from their ordeal, they were adopted into loving homes. The family who adopted "Hero Cat" named her Scarlett.

I wrote this story to honor the tenth anniversary of Scarlett's heroic deed.

—*Eileen Spinelli*

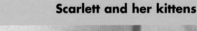

Scarlett and her kittens

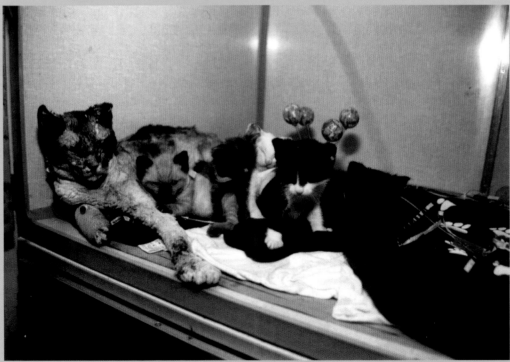

Mary Bloom, *North Shore Animal League America*